Discover Beaverton

Printed in the United States of America.

ISBN: 978-1-956076-05-9

PROOFREADING and CREATIVE DIRECTION by NaBeela Washington
COVER ART and ISSUE DESIGN by Stacey Zhu
GUEST EDITING by Katherine Quevedo

Stacey Zhu is an Illustrator studying at ArtCenter College of Design and is interested in capturing the mundane moments in life.

Katherine Quevedo hails from Beaverton, Oregon, where she works as an analyst and lives with her husband and sons. Her writing has been nominated for the Pushcart Prize and Rhysling Award. Her stories and poems appear or are forthcoming in *Asimov's*, *Fireside*, *Nightmare*, *F&SF*, *On Spec*, *Apparition Lit*, and elsewhere.

Publication of *Discover Beaverton* is made possible through the Beaverton Arts Project Grant, funded by the City of Beaverton Arts Program.

Donate or submit to *Lucky Jefferson* on our website: luckyjefferson.com.

Foreword

In Italo Calvino's *Invisible Cities*, a fictionalized Marco Polo admits, "Every time I describe a city I am saying something about Venice." In my case, I could make the same admission about Beaverton, Oregon. Something about a hometown comes to define those who inhabit it, whether by the circumstances of their upbringing or by their choices as an adult. In my case, Beaverton chose me, as it is where I was born and raised, and I chose it in turn as the place where I would establish my own family. The city shapes us as we go about our daily lives, dining out, attending events, immersing ourselves in nature. It becomes a lens through which we interpret other destinations, near and far, and come to a deeper understanding of our literal and figurative place in the world.

From its origins as the home of the Indigenous Atfalati tribe, to its incorporation as a city in 1893, Beaverton has metamorphosed into a thriving Pacific Northwest community, home to one of Oregon's most diverse populations. It encompasses the world headquarters of not one but two major active apparel companies, a solid representation of the high-tech industry workforce, plus a flourishing hub of arts, entertainment, and cuisine. With this mix of innovation, creativity, and inclusivity at its core, it's no wonder the city has grown so much in recent years.

Beaverton has maintained its natural beauty throughout this evolution. Many of its place-names reflect the foresty ecosystem—Cedar Hills, Five Oaks, Greenway. The list goes on. The city boasts a relatively mild climate (assuming you can handle plenty of rain), yet has four distinct seasons. It's well situated for day trips to the scenic Pacific coast, snowy Mount Hood, big city life in Portland, hiking in the Columbia Gorge, or a longer trek out to Oregon's high desert. Of course, you don't have to leave the city limits to enjoy rolling green hills, the bigleaf maples that shed their huge namesakes in the fall, and wetlands teeming with birds and other wildlife.

My experience of Beaverton is but one of many. Within the pages of this anthology, you are invited to step into the perspectives of some of the city's local writers and artists, or those who have a connection with our community, to immerse yourself in the sites, landmarks, and businesses that give my hometown its many complex layers. This is no invisible city. I am no Marco Polo. You needn't journey far for this adventure of discovery. You need only turn the page…

Katherine Quevedo
Guest Editor

Discover Beaverton With

Rodney Wilder
Beatless in Beaverton

Derek R. Smith
The Crick

Ruth Mota
Summer Blossom

Rhienna Guedry
Crows of the Willamette Valley

Elizabeth Beechwood
Jane Austen in the Beaverton City Library

April Hernandez
Second Home

A.M. Arndt

Home to Nest

Katie Briggs

Thursdays at Ex Novo

Kate Tomich

Hidden Things

Andria Lishka

Farmers Market Fantasy

Marie Queen

High Tea Under the Dirigible Take 1 & 2
(Clockwork Rose Tea Emporium)

Artwork by: Abby Greenplate
Literary Illustrator Intern
abbygreenplate.myportfolio.com

Beatless in Beaverton

Rodney Wilder

Here's a thing I miss that, for once,
has nothing to do with quarantine.
I miss Everyday Music. Specifically,
the squished-betwixt-a-sex-shop-&-
Pita Pit, Cedar Hills location. Its
hors d'oeurve of Old Beaverton. Its
feral-cat bastion of vintagehood,
DIYing while Beaverton Mall re-
brands but continues its DI-dying
across the street.
                    In this suburb that
shutters record stores like a spiteful
younger sibling, jewel cases made
shuriken & shrapnel in its
self-defeating tantrum
against Portland's
shared stock,
where else
to sate this sonivorous craving
but Everyday Music?
Last pin standing that it was,
where else to go bowling for soup or
pan nickel creeks for nuggets of gold-
finger ever one CD away from what
chthonic cure I might find to
eminem floetry from out my
bad brains? I miss
the way my fingertips would begin
their anticipatory divining before I'd
even crossed the threshold, like
   Lo, ye ten ravenous gods. Behold
how the fruit doth quiver. How time
to partake is yours.

It didn't matter
if, just the week before, I had
plundered its plethoras & added
Fugees, Dimmu Borgir,
& the soundtrack to Disney's
The Hunchback of Notre Dame
to my dragon-hoard. (And damn if
that does not say a
poem's worth about me
in & of itself.)
Because
no other record store before or since
has Indiana Jonesed me like that one.
That succulent temple. That
wonderland of redesired media
where the wolves that are nostalgia &
musicophilia both sank their teeth in
& went to sleep.
That garage-sale melange that got
snuck out of its lease by a liquor store.
That reason for spiteful sobriety.
That quaint sadness whenever
in the neighborhood and without
any reason to stay.
There are, of course,
other locations. Other, in-Portland
sticks to scratch this itch with. And,
occasionally, I'll drag my
now-emaciated wolves to their altars
of unrotation & cost, &
nudge them to eat.
They always leave hungry though.
They always leave hungry.

About

Rodney Wilder

Rodney Wilder (he/him) is a biracially-Black nerd with work appearing in places like Half Mystic, Bareknuckle Poet, and Anti-Heroin Chic, as well as Stiltzkin's Quill, his most recent attempt at grimoiring all the geeky incense left lit in his ribcage. Find him on Instagram at @thebardofhousewilder and Twitter at @LilBabyIfrit.

What inspired you to submit to "*Discover Beaverton*"?

I grew up in Beaverton and have always held a lot of fondness for the communal, slightly more laid-back vibe I used to and still can find there. I also have been actively writing poetry and performing spoken word for going on 10+ years now. So seeing this call for submissions felt particularly dialed in, for me.

Was this your first time being published?

No.

What do you love about the piece you submitted?

I love how deeply entrenched in its nostalgias and quaintnesses it is. It's a tribute to my favorite used record shop, Everyday Music—a (now defunct) staple of "Old Beaverton" that I and my wife, for years, had an almost-weekly habit of visiting and spending hours poring through their CDs and DVDs. It's a poem that juggles that nostalgia and nerdery and hyperbolic joy while also never losing hold on the concrete anchors behind why those attachments matter. In an age when our communal relics and staples continue to get obsoleted and shuttered, I'm proud of being able to take a few minutes and a couple pages to honor one that meant so much to me. One that has always been synonymous with the feeling and aesthetic of my first and truest hometown.

What's your favorite thing about Beaverton and/or Oregon?

Before its 2018 closure, I probably would have said my favorite thing about Beaverton was Everyday Music (the subject of my included poem). Barring that though, I have to fall back on another element of Beaverton that had just as hefty a hand—if not greater—in shaping who I am today. As can probably be gleaned from my poem, I'm a nerd. And as an anime-watching, video-gaming, cosplaying, con-going nerd living in the Beaverton area, the city always had a couple key fixtures for those summers when I found myself prepping for an anime convention and working on cosplay: Mill End and Uwajimaya. There is a verifiable magic in spending time hunting for cosplay materials at Mill End and then popping across the parking lot for a victory lap/Japanese snack haul at Uwajimaya. That these two businesses exist as neighbors is precisely what I mean when I say Beaverton had an "it" that cannot be understated. Certainly a magical, very Beaverton-y kind of nostalgia for me.

What are you hoping readers take away from this issue?

I'm hoping readers get a chance to experience just how multifaceted and vast a culture Beaverton had and still has to its name. That's for sure what I'm most excited to experience myself when I get a chance to read it!

What does being a part of this project mean to you?

It is such an incredible feeling to have my hometown spotlit, literarily, and to actually be one of the voices included in crafting that spotlight. There's just nothing like it.

The Crick
Derek R. Smith

Where the hip hop beats drop
Like biscuit dough on a hot griddle
And a person could lose their worries
In reflections of fine Pinot.

A place of spice and character
A feeling like you've been before
On your first stumble
through the threshold:

The warm hello and priceless
perfume of plantains,
cornbread, and
the summa plate—ha.

You bring a friend or twelve
You grab a wine or dozen
And Mr. Bertony shares a joke
That almost reminds you of someone
But no, they are gone now.

And they would have loved this spot.
It's a place between places,
And it evokes all the NOLA charms,
Every family gathering for its volume,
It's here where you are the exact thing
That was missing
Just a moment ago.

The intention and the effortless
Of your new favorite place to be
You'll carry home a wine glass
Etched with old school headphones
That embrace a bottle,
You are capturing warm summer sun
In mason jars full of homemade strawberry jam.

There's a strength of character
In this grape ship in a bottle,
Just take a sip
Then close your eyes
And let the tunes and
Tannins take you
Where you need.

About

Derek R. Smith

Derek R. Smith is a public health professional, Anishinaabe two-spirit, uncle, sibling, friend, who writes poetry on paper scraps. He has 2023 publications in Great Lakes Review, ¡Pa'lante!, San Antonio Review, euphony, and Ignatian Literary Magazine. There is no space for distance here, in poetry, and isn't that a beautiful thing?

What inspired you to submit to "*Discover Beaverton*"?

I am a poet for fun, I work in public health for my paid gig. The opportunity seemed so curious and so fun!

Was this your first time being published?

No.

What do you love about the piece you submitted?

I like that describing a place calls on us to evoke all the senses. I wanted to describe what you hear, what your heart feels, what you smell, all the feelings that come with being somewhere cool and inviting. It's sort of a love poem. We all like to find places where we can be ourselves, meet new people, simply relax and rejuvenate in the best of humanity.

What's your favorite thing about Beaverton and/or Oregon?

Oregon is still newer to me after 4 years living here. But it's where my family is. It's where there are always hikes. It's a magic place in summer. The spring and most of the year is green, green, living. The winter can be harder, but it's a great time to write, to find new gathering places, to go a bit internal and restore while we dream about the garden we will plant and the adventure we will take.

What are you hoping readers take away from this issue?

I truly hope it's a bunch of love poems. Using poetry to describe a community and exploring important spaces is such a great journey. I look forward to reading the issue. I wonder if people will read something about a well-known favorite spot, and see it in a truly different light after reading what was contributed about it. It's a wonderful thing to see something old through a new lens. I believe every part of this project invites us all to take a beat, open ourselves in a new way, and express gratitude for the things big and small that we love.

What does being a part of this project mean to you?

This project called for us all to think about favorite local spaces in a new way, to reconsider places we spend time at but don't always take the time to honor and appreciate. I love the new view of these places, the love letters to favorite local spots on the map of Beaverton. The writing project brings into words a novel way of thinking about the places and spaces that matter to us. The assignment pulled together support for small business, uplifting the arts, and love for community.

Summer Blossom

Ruth Mota

We spilled into our white whale of a Buick -
mom, dad, our collie Shek and I. From the suburbs
of San Francisco to grandma's farm in Beaverton,
we whizzed by hard gray blocks of city to soft tilled land
metered out in billboards and Burma Shave ditties.
My father had me name the crops we passed and cities
starting with the letter "M" that had a million population:
Minneapolis, Moscow, Melbourne, Madrid...
Time and distance shrank as the world expanded
until our dog awoke all ears and whimpers
to the tire-crunch of gravel on Route 2.

A fir branch had fallen on our log cabin
so I spent my first day upon the roof
nailing shingles my father handed me.
High above the rows of corn and beans,
I saw my grandma hoeing in a fury,
her grip fierce as barbed wire,
mouth tight as a dress seam.

Shek romped and sniffed beneath the honeysuckle
while mother picked pails of cherries.
After work, these Bings would stain
my lips and fingers before I spit their pits
in lofty arches on the loamy soil and wondered
which, if any, might give birth.

At night, bone-weary, I climbed up to the attic with my lantern.
Shek slept beside the metal bed, wound like a bagel, paws twitching
in some dreamy rabbit chase on grandma's rug of braided rags.
I curled beneath my quilt by the open window,
listened to cricket chirps swallow up the stillness.
The singing night air unfurled like a black tongue
beyond the house, beyond the trees,
beyond the spinning stars.

I floated so far into the dizzying darkness
I failed to feel the crimson
blossom on my sheet.

About

Ruth Mota

Ruth currently lives in the Santa Cruz Mountains of California where she focuses on writing poetry or facilitating poetry circles to groups in her community. Her poems have been published in many online and print journals including: Cathexis Northwest, High Shelf Press, Gyroscope Review, Terrapin Books and Canary Literary Journal among others.

What inspired you to submit to "*Discover Beaverton*"?

I am a retired international health trainer currently living in the Santa Cruz Mountains of California, now devoted to writing poetry. My poems have been published in many online and print journals. I discovered your call for poems on submittable and I had previously written this one, which had never been published, about one of my summers on my grandmother's farm in Beaverton.

Was this your first time being published?

No.

What do you love about the piece you submitted?

Our visits to the Beaverton farm when I entered puberty in the 1950s were magical for me. The log cabin had an attic full of my grandmother's treasures: quilts and rugs she made, photos of her in a long skirt on an antiquated bicycle, the long black braid she cut when bobbing hair became the fashion. Besides the victory garden she planted, there was a forest lined with trilliums that led to a creek where we swam. She pumped water and chopped kindling for the wood stove into her nineties. I was born in Oregon where my father was head of elementary school education for the state until he was recruited to be superintendent of the Palo Alto schools in California. So these retreats to the farm were special times when he took off his city veneer and the family bonded.

What's your favorite thing about Beaverton and/or Oregon?

During my youth I loved my mother's stories of Mt Hood. Her name was Thelma. She and her best friend, Louise, taught at the one-room school at the base of the mountain and at 18 went on horseback from Mt Hood to Mt Jefferson running into sheep rustlers and having other adventures along the way.

What are you hoping readers take away from this issue?

I hope that those who live in Beaverton love it as much as I did as a child, now that it has grown into a lovely city. I hope, from my poem, they get a glimpse of its prior life.

What does being a part of this project mean to you?

I am honored to be part of this project.

Artwork by: Ati Gor
Literary Illustrator Intern
aticor.carrd.co

Crows of the Willamette Valley

Rhienna Guedry

We woke up early first
Stayed up late second

This is how we learned
When the fog comes in and

Where you went after:
Tree-top committee

Your neighborhood watch
I, too, have been paying attention

To distrustful men and fresh road kill
Ribbon prisms, complex as rainbows

Yours a brassy confidence of staying put
(If only you could invite me to crow court)

Instead, I place an offering
On the one dry day in May, you

Swoop down from a tree that holds you over
Land we live on but know better than to say we own

About

Rhienna Guedry

Rhienna Renée Guedry (she/they) is a writer, illustrator, and producer whose favorite geographic locations all have something to do with their proximity to water. A two-time Pushcart Prize nominee and 2022 Tin House Workshop alum, her work has appeared in Muzzle, Maudlin House, Gigantic Sequins, and elsewhere. Her debut chapbook Root Rot is available from Cooper Dillon Books. Rhienna is currently working on her first novel. Find out more about her projects at rhienna.com.

What inspired you to submit to "*Discover Beaverton*"?

Writer and sometimes artist, I'm always looking for the intersection between my local community and the larger creative one, and this call and publication sounded exciting.

Was this your first time being published?

No.

What do you love about the piece you submitted?

I got really into birds, especially in the past 3-5 years. It's not fair to say I have favorites, but the crows here get a lot of my attention. This is a love poem for them.

What's your favorite thing about Beaverton and/or Oregon?

I love getting lost. What I mean by that is, I love a detour, taking a route or road that runs generally where I'm headed and see what happens. This is especially significant by bike, when I'm rarely going very fast and can pay close attention to so many things: cute dogs, a piece of street art, surprising decor on someone's front porch, someone unseen practicing violin, the smell of spices from cooking or grilling.

What are you hoping readers take away from this issue?

Inspiration and appreciation.

What does being a part of this project mean to you?

It's easy to feel disconnected from a cultural center outside of institutions like universities, museums, writing intensive workshops, even bookstores. Publications and initiatives like this help focus locals to be in conversation with one another, and hopefully give local readers something to look forward to and be proud of. Thank you!

Home To Nest

A.M. Arndt

The birds have come home to nest for the spring;
along Deschutes and Columbia curves,
over crumbling rock cliffs and waterfalls,
through alfalfa hay and wheat fields,
they have flown their feathers homeward.

The birds are everywhere come springtime:
Meadowlarks lead local songbirds in sunrise sings,
which give way, in the later day, to falcon cries.
Larger birds of prey arc radial rainbows across the sky,
wings wide, while below,
the quail and pheasant, afoot, run wild.
At night, the wisest huntress, Owl, reigns the realm,
a silent, watchful presence in the velvet dark.

The birds have come home to nest for the spring;
along Pacific Coast and Cascade crests,
over Wanapum glyphs and Celilo tribal lands,
through outstretched orchard limbs and reaching vines,
they have flown their feathers homeward.

The birds have come home to nest for the spring;
Red-winged Blackbird, Mountain Bluebird,
Grassland Yellow Finch, and Purple Martin
are flashes of feather,
flowers in the greening landscape.

The birds have come home to nest for the spring.

About

A.M. Arndt

A.M. Arndt is an Oregon educator and writer of, mostly, free verse poetry. This poet has been recognized by the Dorothy Sargent Rosenberg Poetry Contest, has had the poem "Hemingway" published in Into the Void out of Dublin, Ireland and the poem "French Press" published in Capsule Stories.

What inspired you to submit to "*Discover Beaverton*"?

I am a writer, and are you kidding me? What an opportunity to be able to submit work about places that I love and that speak to me. I have lived in Oregon since just before I turned 12, and I have a deep love for many places in the state. One of the things I appreciate about Beaverton is its mix of glass and greenery; it's certainly an Oregon city: a jungle of wildlife and concrete.

Was this your first time being published?

No

What do you love about the piece you submitted?

My father asked me about my writing process, which I hadn't ever had to put into words for someone. Once I explained, he paused and then requested a poem about birds. I think, initially, I laughed, but what better way to express thoughts about Oregon than through its wildlife? Thus, "Home to Nest" was born.

What's your favorite thing about Beaverton and/or Oregon?

Sense memories are powerful and Oregon boasts a bounty of places that will make one recall the tastes, sights, smells, and adventures of a specific place with uncanny clarity. One of my favorite sense memories from a backpacking trip to Bear Lake was the smell of wild huckleberry as the sun warmed the woods. It was like walking into Grandmother's kitchen.

What are you hoping readers take away from this issue?

Oregon is as diverse as its people. This is worth celebrating. This is worth promoting.

What does being a part of this project mean to you?

Authors write and artists create because they have to. They will create whether or not they are recognized because the drive to do so is within them, but the dream is that someone could look at the work that has been created and identify with it, relate to it in some way. It is a great honor to have one's work resonate with an audience. In a world that is so quick to point out differences, when someone connects to a writer or artist's work, it is an extension of that human connection. Creating these connections should concern all of us much more than our differences.

Artwork by: Abby Greenplate
Literary Illustrator Intern
abbygreenplate.myportfolio.com

Jane Austen In The Beaverton City Library

Elizabeth Beechwood

Hello, my name is Jane Austen.
I'm not a famous writer, but I do work with books.

I live in the Beaverton City Library, in a cozy nest I built inside the wall of a room where library staff do behind-the-scenes work. I consider myself an honorary librarian, assisting patrons as well.

It wasn't always this way. When I was younger, I moved out of my mother's crowded nest in search of a place to call my own. My journey brought me to a grassy area filled with people going in and out of a glass and brick building, speaking different languages, laughing, and smiling. I knew whatever was inside that building was welcoming to those people. I wondered, would it be welcoming to one small mouse who needed a place to call her own? There weren't any barriers or steps to climb, so it was easy enough for me to sneak in and…

What a wonderous place opened up before me—a place I'd never imagined could exist!

It took me a year to explore every inch of the library, to find the perfect place for my nest, to explore all the shelves. By the time that year was over, I'd fallen in love with the library staff and the patrons who came in regularly. I'd fallen in love with reading and learning new things every day. I fell in love with my little nest and the wide open second floor that made me feel like I was outside but never wet or cold.

And, yet, something was still missing in my life. Something I couldn't quite put my paw on.

One morning, I was exploring the non-fiction section when I heard a sniffle. I peeked over the neatly shelved books and saw a woman in a red shirt and jeans wiping her eyes. She took one book off the shelf, skimmed through it, then replaced it. Then she took another, looked at it and tucked it under her arm. She wiped her eyes again and blew her nose. My little heart sank as I watched her. I knew what section she was searching through.

For the first time, it hit me that the library wasn't just for fun things like poetry readings or finding the perfect book to learn how to knit. It was about getting good information into the hands of people who needed it.

I felt a little foolish for having taken so long to realize that. But this was an opportunity. How many times had I seen library staff help patrons find what they were looking for? Direct them to the correct website? Suggest resources? Thoughts raced through my mind: Should I run and find one of the library staff? What would I do to get them to this patron? How could I, a small mouse who needed to stay hidden, help this woman?

The woman wiped her eyes again and headed down the aisle, away from the book I knew she needed. I had to act fast.

I bolted down one shelf, picked out the book and gave it a push with my shoulder. Nothing. I pushed with both my front paws. Nothing. I turned around and pushed with my back but couldn't get good leverage on the slick metal shelf. I poked my head over the book; she was nearly out of the aisle. I gave it one last heave with all my might and intention.

And it worked! The book slid out from its spot on the shelf and onto the floor with a satisfying thump that caught the woman's attention. She turned, saw the book, and looked around. I couldn't help myself—I peeked through the gap in the books and whispered, "This is the book you need."

She picked up Chicken Soup for the Soul: The Cancer Book and read the cover, read the back, glanced inside. Then she smiled and looked up at the ceiling.

"Thank you," she said.

"You're welcome," I whispered back when she was too far away to hear me.

That's when I knew that I, too, could help no matter how small I was or how unseen I needed to remain.

My next opportunity came with a teenaged boy standing in the doorway to the Teen Center. He walked back and forth, like he really wanted to go in but just couldn't make himself do it. I recognized the symbol on his green t-shirt—the same symbol I'd seen on comic books and several of the other teens' t-shirts. He was so close. If he'd only step into that room, he'd find so many books and friends.

I scrambled over the shelves to the comics near him. The comic book was a lot easier to push off the shelf and I nearly fell out after it. Just as I'd hoped, the boy saw it and walked over and picked it up. Some other teens saw the book fall, too.

"That's so weird," one of them said. "It's like that book jumped out just for you." The shy teen smiled just a bit.

"I love that series, too. Have your read the third one yet? It's great."

And then they were all discussing comic books and the teenaged boy seemed to have forgotten about being nervous.

Then there was the young girl who was having a difficult time finding a book with characters who looked like her, until I pushed it off the shelf for her. Or the frazzled dad who, while chasing twins through the kids' section, discovered a parenting book on the floor right next to the dinosaur books his kids loved to sit and look at.

My opportunities to help are endless.

The next time you're in the Beaverton City Library and a book falls next to you or you find yourself in a section you didn't even know you needed, think of me, Jane Austen, the library mouse. I'm always ready to help even if you don't see me.

About

Elizabeth Beechwood

Elizabeth Beechwood lives west of Portland, Oregon, with her two cats and too many plants. She's a graduate of USM's Stonecoast MFA Program and her work has been published in the award-winning anthology "Nox Pareidolia", Third Flatiron's "Hidden Histories", and Not a Pipe Publishing's "Strongly Worded Women" anthology.

What inspired you to submit to "*Discover Beaverton*"?

I'm a writer who loves setting my stories in familiar places and then watching them take off in strange directions. Beaverton is a place I know well, so writing a story set in the library seemed like a natural starting point!

Was this your first time being published?

No.

What do you love about the piece you submitted?

I love Miss Jane Austen, mouse librarian! If a book falls next to you in the library, you should definitely pick it up and read it.

What's your favorite thing about Beaverton and/or Oregon?

What I love most about Oregon is that you can drive from the ocean, through a valley, over a mountain, and into a high desert in one day. Libraries are particularly magical places where everyone is welcome.

What are you hoping readers take away from this issue?

Everyone can help others in their own special way.

What does being a part of this project mean to you?

This project has given me the opportunity to share the magic of Beaverton, and libraries, with my community and beyond through my writing.

Thursdays at Ex Novo

Katie Briggs

Date night is usually on a Thursday.
A steaming Philip the Black pizza. Salad with fruit and feta. Beers for two.
Plants and succulents scattered between kind smiles.
Most know our order.
Some know our names.
Barrel-top tables the perfect size for a game of cards.
We eat. We breathe.
Date night is usually on a Thursday.

About

Katie Briggs

Katie has lived in Beaverton since 2006. She loves the farmers market, downtown, and the easy access she has to Portland and the coast. Katie can often be found behind a book in a coffee shop or on a pickleball court trying to figure out her backhand.

What inspired you to submit to "*Discover Beaverton*"?

Beaverton deserves to be celebrated, so when I saw an opportunity to help do that, I was curious. Then I clicked on the "Beaverton Scavenger Map" and saw Ex Novo Brewing on the list. It was time to put pen to paper.

Was this your first time being published?

Yes.

What do you love about the piece you submitted?

I love the line "Plants and succulents scattered between kind smiles." Ex Novo has such a welcoming and friendly atmosphere and my hope is to give readers the same feeling. For readers who haven't experienced Ex Novo, you should also know that the pizza and beer are fantastic–any day of the week.

What's your favorite thing about Beaverton and/or Oregon?

Beaverton's offerings and location make it an amazing place to live! It's an inclusive, evolving city with an expanding food and culture scene. And we have easy access to the beautiful Oregon coast, the mountains, and Soccer City USA (AKA Portland). I feel blessed to call Beaverton home.

What are you hoping readers take away from this issue?

My hope is that readers are inspired to explore the many amazing places and events that Beaverton has to offer.

What does being a part of this project mean to you?

I love Beaverton. Being a part of an artistic endeavor that highlights what makes it so lovable is a privilege. Thank you for including me.

Second Home

April Hernandez

Picture this: *A small child wearing her thrifted pink Paul Frank tee paired with black leggings and light-up pink and white tennis shoes holds her grandmother's hand as they enter the Wilshire Market, their neighborhood convenience store. They approach the counter, and the grandmother pulls some cash out of her purse. She asks for lottery tickets, one for each jackpot. As the cashier rings up the transaction, the grandmother glances down at the child who is keeping herself occupied by humming the Three's Company theme song. The grandmother bends down and whispers something into the child's ear that causes her to giggle with delight. The child then skips toward a sliding door freezer, her long, thick dark brown hair swishing back and forth. She skips back to her grandmother with two piña con chile paletas in hand and a big, toothy smile on her face. The grandmother pays for the popsicles and the lottery tickets and the two exit the store, holding hands and eating their tasty treats.*

The scene described above is one I am familiar with, as that little girl was me. I have a lot of memories of spending time with my grandparents before I was old enough to go to school, and sometimes when I was well-behaved while accompanying them as they ran errands, they would treat me to a paleta or an ice cream cone. Now that I'm in my late twenties and both of my grandparents have passed away, I can't help but reminisce about little moments like the one I described whenever I have a paleta or some other Mexican treat. While Portland is a city filled with diverse cuisines, I've found that usually, the suburbs of the Portland area are the best places to find (in my opinion) the better and more authentic Mexican panaderías and such. Therefore, I don't indulge in the Mexican goodies as much as I probably would if the locations were closer to where I live, but when I do get the opportunity to have them I am abuzz with happiness and nostalgia.

**

(May 2023) My partner Gabriel and I hold hands as we enter through the door of Ome Calli, a nevería and paletería located in Beaverton, Oregon. I immediately feel like I am that little girl again and eagerly let my eyes drink in the labels for the plethora of traditional Mexican ice cream and paleta flavors like chamoy, mango, horchata, and arroz con leche. When I approach the counter I instinctively look over my shoulder, almost as if I am expecting to see my grandparents standing there and nodding their permission for me to order myself a frozen delicacy. Instead, I find Gabe's smiling cerulean eyes peering down at me. I grin at him before I turn back to the server and place my order: a piña con chile paleta. Just like old times. I pay for my paleta and Gabe's strawberry paleta and we make our way outside. We trade bites and agree that the spice of the chile mixed with the tanginess of the pineapple is incredibly refreshing in the late May heat. We quickly devour our treats before they melt and make our way back to the car holding hands once again.

"Ome Calli" is from the indigenous Mexican language Nahuatl and translates to "Second Home." I think this is the perfect name for the business, since it represents the owners' history of calling both Mexico and Oregon their home. However, I also think that "Ome Calli" is a perfect name for my own experience. Before, my grandparents were the "home" of a lot of the Mexican traditions that I grew up with, including the love of paletas. Now that I am grown and have built my life with Gabe, he and I are the "home" of our own traditions that consist of those from our respective childhoods as well as those that we've begun together. While he may not have the same palate that I developed courtesy of growing up in a Mexican-American household, he does appreciate having pan dulce and paletas every so often, so I am happy that we can keep that tradition alive.

About

April Hernandez

April Alexis Hernandez is a Portland, Oregon native and the Co-Coordinator of Pile Press. Her CNF chapbook *Getting to Know the Stoveman* (Bottlecap Press) was published this year, and she had the opportunity to read excerpts from it at Powell's Smallpresspalooza 2023. Follow her on Instagram @april.alexis.

What inspired you to submit to "*Discover Beaverton*"?

I am a writer from the Portland area, and I had a poem titled "Dementia" that was nominated for a Pushcart Prize by Lucky Jefferson. When I saw the announcement for Discover Beaverton, I knew I wanted to write something for it.

Was this your first time being published?

No.

What do you love about the piece you submitted?

I haven't written as much as I would like to in recent years because I have been busy in other areas of life and in the writing space, so I love this piece because it is one of the newest pieces of writing that I've worked on in a long time. I really appreciate that Lucky Jefferson is including it in this issue.

What's your favorite thing about Beaverton and/or Oregon?

I think my favorite thing about Oregon is that there are so many different terrains that are easily accessible. In just a few hours you could be at the beach, or the mountains, or the gorge, or the desert, or the forest, or the city...there is so much to do in just one state and I feel so fortunate to live here.

What are you hoping readers take away from this issue?

I hope that readers are able to see how special Beaverton (and Oregon) is. I've lived in Portland all my life and growing up, Beaverton didn't always feel like it was a very diverse place. I'm happy to see that things have changed and that Beaverton is celebrating its diversity, its cultures and its art. I hope that readers can see that and will consider visiting the area to experience it for themselves.

What does being a part of this project mean to you?

As a lifelong Oregonian, I feel so honored to be included in a project that celebrates the state as well as the Beaverton community. This project is such a great opportunity to showcase what we have to offer and to highlight areas that others may be less familiar with.

Farmers Market Fantasy

Andria Lishka

Stella held Daddy's hand ahead of me with Sam in the wagon. We crossed the rectangle park across from the Beaverton Library. The splash pad was going. Sam wanted to run through it now, but Stella reminded him of gelato, returning his focus to getting into the market proper.

Wafts of scent–brewing coffee and kettle corn–drifted over the crowded aisles. Music from a live band filled the air.

After two flats of strawberries, a satchel of peppers, and a potted fuchsia were in the wagon, Sam got out, offering to pull. We'd turned into the aisle of art and craft stalls. I looked for my husband's tall frame ahead of us. He and Stella had disappeared.

"They went in there, Mommy." Sam pointed to the sparkly black drapes of Engineer Dan's Whistle-Stop. "I hear locomotives, let's go in too!"

The sign wasn't much to go on for what to expect, but locomotives? If I strained my ears, I heard them too. It was likely homemade toys, and Stella would've dragged Daddy in. Once I heard the trains, I couldn't unhear them. I was half convinced I'd been hearing steam locomotive noises all morning. We stepped in, still pulling the wagon. I didn't know what to expect, but a life-size British Victorian train station, complete with tracks, was not it.

The day outside the tent had been sunny warm Oregon summer. Here, the sky was overcast and rainy. The asphalt roadway of the Farmers Market had turned to cobblestones. Wet grit under my Birkenstock sandals scraped as I looked back.

A rectangle of normal goings-on at the market could be seen. My shorts and tee shirt, perfect for where I'd been, left me chilly here.

"Mommy! It's Thomas!" Sam shouted. He dropped the handle and ran for the platform beside the tracks. Sure enough, a blue steam engine came puffing up to the station, with the anthropomorphic face on the front of the steam barrel.

One last look behind me at the market, and home, then I grabbed the wagon handle as I followed Sam.

Daddy and Stella were on the platform excitedly exchanging notes with Sam on the accuracy of this world to the show they were so familiar with.

"Dad?" I shot my husband a look, "What is going on here?"

He shrugged and said, "I don't think we can leave without taking a ride."

"All aboard!" the locomotive, er, Thomas shouted. "All aboard for the Circle Line. Ride lasts twenty minutes and brings you right back here." The tone in Thomas' voice spoke volumes. He'd been asked that a lot.

We boarded a coach and found plain wooden benches beside windows. A few other families from Beaverton had found their way in here, wearing summer clothes, and bemused expressions. There were people who fit this world too, wearing wool skirts or trousers, in dour colors. We seemed to have stepped into a bit of British history and they gave us newcomers grumpy looks.

I'd left our wagon on the platform and was surprised to see some station workers loading it on a flat car behind the coach.

Thomas chugged out of the station, and Stella and Sam were ecstatic, pointing out the window as we steamed along.

Cows grazing in the rain, flocks of sheep mowing the hillside, their white backs a contrast to the deep greens of the pastures around them. Thomas had a way of amplifying his voice into the passenger cars. He spoke about adventures in staying on schedule, while not hitting any wandering sheep.

The tour ended as Thomas pulled back into the Victorian station saying, "I hope you enjoyed your trip to the Island of Sodor. Please don't leave anything behind, retrieving it later won't be possible."

We exited the passenger coach and started for the edge of the platform. One of the station workers with a ledger book stopped me. He had our market wagon too.

"Here's your bill of goods, Madam. Please sign your receipts."

I did, and he handed me that, and the handle of the wagon, then bid us good day and returned to his work. A new crowd of bemused summer-clothed people were on the platform.

At the edge of the cobbled area, we found the rectangle of normality that we'd left.

"Mommy! We got to ride on Thomas! I got to talk to Thomas!" Sam's excitement was bubbling out of him.

I smiled down as he put his hand in mine. "Yes, it was a very nice surprise."

We stepped out into the bustle of the Farmers Market, and I turned back to look where we'd been. The tent was still there, with the sign proclaiming Engineer Dan's Whistle-Stop, but the sparkly black drapes were tied back. Hand-carved wooden toy train tracks were on the tables. Bright wooden locomotives were being pushed by excited children, their parents standing back as they played. In the middle of the table was a small wood model of a Victorian-style train station, with little wood figures of people and workers gathered on the platform.

Paper rustled in my hand. I'd forgotten I'd taken the receipt of my own wagon a few minutes ago. I looked closer at the page, and under the list, "strawberries, blueberries, peppers, plant, and wagon," there was my signature, on an old-fashioned receipt for Sodor Railways.

I read it three times, fingering the flimsy page, then feeling eyes on me, I looked up. Engineer Dan himself caught my eye. He was wearing British work overalls and a tam-o-shanter hat with an Island of Sodor pin. With a secret kind of smile and a knowing inside-joke wink, he acknowledged my unspoken question with a nod.

"Mommy?" Sam looked up from the train table. "Can we go get gelato now?"

"Yeah, can we get gelato?" Stella seconded.

I returned the wink, gathered my family, and said, "Sure! It's a lot hotter here than it was on the train!"

About

Andria Lishka

Andria Lishka has lived in Beaverton since 1998. She teaches in Portland Public Schools. Her children grew up here, her husband works for Intel, and she love animals (horses, dogs and dragons) writing, reading, making miniatures, travel, movies and music, not necessarily in that order.

What inspired you to submit to "*Discover Beaverton*"?

I've lived in Beaverton for about twenty-five years now, my children have grown up here. I had lived other places (born in Berkeley, CA. Spent teens and early twenties in Madison, Wisconsin. Married and spent 1991-1998 living in/around Geneva, Switzerland) before landing here in Beaverton (1998 to present). My daughter was born in Geneva, and my son born here in Oregon.

I am more of a writer, but I do draw, create miniatures, dollhouses and vignette rooms and other small things—LEGOs, limited origami, I can sew (given a pattern, and sometimes just inventing as I go). I love horses, dogs and dragons. I love to read (Anne McCaffery is a long time favorite). I like to play World of Warcraft (a guilty pleasure for 17 years now). I love Science Fiction and Fantasy, movies, good TV shows, music and concerts. I love to write, I have self-published a Fantasy story (which took forever to write) and World of Warcraft fan-fiction on Archive of Our Own—both under the name "AM Fox" (my last name means fox in Czech, so it's a pretty close to the truth nom-de-plume). I have been part of a local writer's group, on and off since 1999, and we share and support each other in writing—some of us have even published for real! I'm about to join the ranks of "published for real," and I'm very excited about that!

I went back to school in 2008, and earned a Masters in Education (MED) from PSU by 2016; currently I am an Educational Assistant in a Portland Public School. I love to serve and give back to my community, and I love working with kids—my position last academic year was in 4th grade, next fall, I'll be working with 5th graders.

So what inspired me to contribute a submission to Discover Beaverton? It was a chance to write a fun short piece that tapped into a time when my kids were very young. We've always enjoyed going to Farmers Market in downtown Beaverton in the summers. The splash pad is irresistible on summer days, and my kids loved it. I've always loved the "artist's row" in the Farmer's Market, and felt this was an opportunity to give it a bit of mystery and fun besides all the wonderful pottery, art, handy crafts, jewelry and toy stalls that you can usually find there.

Was this your first time being published?

Yes.

What do you love about the piece you submitted?

When my son was under the age of six, he really, REALLY, enjoyed playing with wooden toy trains (Thomas and Friends) and would lay out crazy- huge track layouts all over our family room floor. These would stay in place for days (or until I insisted we needed to vacuum the carpet) and he and his sister would play and argue over scenario of the day (or hour, sometimes) from morning until dinnertime in the summer.

A longer version of this story includes a bit about how the kids had used the main character's family room floor for a train track layout and would use the furniture as landscape obstacles. One year (early 2000's) my family and I went out to Mt. Hood Railroad, where "Thomas" had come to visit- and they had a full, life-size mock up of Thomas to pull their passenger cars on short rides up and down their railway there- my son was entranced.

So, fast-forward eighteen or so years, something clicked when I heard about a chance to submit a story about living here. My ideas started with, "hmm, farmer's market, and something magical happens in the art row..." and narrowed down to what is Farmer's Market to me? A chance to do things with family no matter who you are, and an experience you can participate in, or not as you choose. Anyone could put themselves in that family's place; they may have chosen a different magical tent, but wooden toy trains are fairly universal in their appeal to boys, girls and parents, and I had that kernel of true experience to wrap it all around too. Write what you know, even it if is fantasy, and it will be better for it!

What's your favorite thing about Beaverton and/or Oregon?

I have had twenty-five years of exploring, and visiting places in around Oregon, and it has so many wonderful places to visit.

I really love the coast of Oregon—something about the wild, windy, sandy and rocky stretch just really speaks to me, and I love it. Pick a spot—it will be beautiful, but I especially love Ecola State Park, between Cannon Beach and Seaside Oregon.

I taught a session of outdoor school for OMSI near Fossil Oregon, and the "ghost" town of Shaniko (which was on the way) has a marvelous outdoor museum and one or two small businesses still open to check out. The Clarno and John Day Fossil beds, arid high desert and Painted Hills are fabulous places to visit and learn more about.

In and around the Hood River area, there is something called the Fruit Loop, where you can drive up and around the hilly area north of Mt Hood, and visit farms to buy fresh produce and products, plus the Mt Hood Railroad (the same company that dressed up one of its engines as Thomas and took my enthralled family on a short jaunt back in the early 2000's) is in the town of Hood River, and they offer tours on their trains, and fun outdoor activities as well as being an operating freight service for farmers up-slope from Hood River to get their goods down to the Columbia river.

And of course Beaverton! We have a wonderful library, right downtown across from the Farmer's Market, we have lovely bike trails and parks galore. There's outdoor movies in the summer in the park near the library (well, pre-pandemic for sure- I'd have to check and see if they're still going before I swore to it). Our parks frequently have concerts to go enjoy live music and socialize too.

What are you hoping readers take away from this issue?

I hope readers of Discover Beaverton will do just that: discover something new about Beaverton and decide to come check it out!

What does being a part of this project mean to you?

I got to share my creativity, tap into my community and share a real weekly event. It means I had the courage to write, speak-up, and share something personal to me. It was read, heard, appreciated, and in-turn, shared with more folks than I could reach by myself, and I love that! May others also have the courage to write, speak, be heard and shared too.

'23

High Tea Under the Dirigible Take 1

(Clockwork Rose Tea Emporium)

Marie Queen

Marie Queen grew up in the Pacific Northwest where she currently resides with her patient husband and two busy daughters. When she is not spending time with family, she enjoys reading, painting, dancing, board-gaming, book-clubbing, drinking pretty drinks, and planning out her big novel.

What inspired you to submit to "*Discover Beaverton*"?

I was inspired to submit to "Discover Beaverton" because I was born, raised, and currently live in Beaverton. I have so many happy memories from here and obviously think it's a great place to live since I chose to move back after college. I am an artist but am also working on my writing.

Was this your first time being published?

Yes.

What do you love about the piece you submitted?

I love the Clockwork Rose Tea Emporium. It's my favorite tea shop in Oregon and may be the only Steampunk tea shop in existence. The hanging dirigible in the tea parlor changes color, and by a happy accident, I captured this transformation on a photo. I then proceeded to sketch and paint a number of paintings based on the photo with my favorite part always being the radiant dirigible. I enjoyed experimenting with different painting/drawing styles and like how my two pieces feel different from each other.

Hidden Things

Kate Tomich

Lydia wiped the sweat from her Ava Roasteria iced caramel macchiato on her shorts, only half-listening to the chatter of her lab partner walking beside her.

"Then I found out there are fairies in Beaverton," Amie said.

"Fairies?" Lydia gave her a side-eyed glance. Amie seemed to be serious, but she always seemed serious about her outlandish stories. "There's no such thing as fairies. Besides, aren't fairies European?"

"They're from their own place, not one of our places. And there is such a thing as fairies."

Lydia raised her eyebrows. "Yeah? How do you know?"

Amie stopped walking and faced Lydia, her gaze solemn and intent. "Don't laugh."

Lydia shifted her drink to her other hand and crossed her heart.

"I met them."

"You met fairies? Where?"

"Behind that stretch of old stores on Farmington, just down from the school."

"There's nothing behind there but more buildings." Lydia started walking again.

"There's a hidden courtyard with a wishing well just off the walkway between those two shops at the end of the row. Come on, I'll show you."

Amie took the lead, heading back toward school on a route that would take them past the string of old buildings. She ducked into a walkway between two of the aged, brown-brick structures, motioning for Lydia to catch up. "I used to walk around a lot when I moved here in September, just checking things out, learning where stuff is. I didn't know anyone yet, so I didn't have anything else to do. I walked down this alley all the time.

There's something mysterious and magical about these little paths between these classic buildings and this whole, older section of town. Makes me feel like I'm in an old movie. Anyhow, one day I saw a little passageway I hadn't seen before. I know now it's because it's not always there. It led to this fabulous little courtyard. Wellhouse in the middle, benches and flowers all around and apartments above the shops with laundry hanging over the railings. It's exactly how I imagine Europe when I think about traveling there."

"I've been down here before," Lydia interrupted. "There's no other alley here, just this one. No courtyard. Maybe you were confused and it was somewhere else?"

Amie shook her head and rolled her eyes. "It's right here." She turned into a narrow lane not even the width of a sidewalk.

Lydia stopped at the entrance. "There was never an alley here."

"It's not always here. Or maybe it is, and you just have to know to look for it."

"And you learned this from fairies?"

"Yes!" Amie was eager again, pulling Lydia's arm to guide her down the path. "In the courtyard, I heard music. I followed it, and I met two of them. They took me down the well. We went to this amazing party, but I can't quite remember it. That's why I want to go back! I know I loved it there. Everything was beautiful. The people, the food, the music. I just want to go back so I can remember it!"

They emerged into the courtyard, and it was just as Amie had described it. The corners were filled with ornate cement planters bursting with climbing roses. Terracotta pots in every size were arrayed on the ground and clustered on wooden platforms and trestles, overflowing with more roses and begonias and other flowers Lydia couldn't name. Reds and pinks and purples and blues crowded together, and the perfume was nearly intoxicating as she breathed it in. A small mermaid fountain surrounded by stone benches burbled in a corner. And in the center was the well house. It looked like a tiny, gray stone cottage with an open front. Inside, Lydia could see the well, made from the same pale gray stone, with a peaked roof over it and a wooden bucket hanging down.

"This is crazy," Lydia said. "How can this be here and I never knew it? I've lived here my whole life!"

"I think they showed it to me because I was so lonely. They said you usually have to give a 'proper gift' to get invited to their parties. They must have felt sorry for me, so they took me with them. Just once, though. I've tried going back. Dropped coins and pretty rocks and even jewelry into the well, but nothing happened. I thought I heard music once, but then it was gone. And I really need to go back!"

Lydia smiled kindly. "I think you were really lonely at the start of the year, and this place does seem magical. I can get why you would think fairies lived here, but..."

"Listen! Do you hear that?"

Lydia leaned over the edge of the well, straining her ears. Faint notes, almost familiar, drifted up to her.

"I hear it!"

"They're down there!" Amie's voice was almost a sob. "I'm so sorry about this, Lydia."

"Sorry? This is so cool! Why are you..." She half-turned back toward Amie, and the other girl shoved against her shoulder, toppling her into the well.

Lydia cried out, but her voice was drowned in the overpowering scent of roses and a swell of heartachingly beautiful music from below. Her plunge slowed, and she opened her eyes. She felt a slim, cool hand in hers.

"You're fine," said a throaty voice near her ear.

Above her, another voice thundered. "This is not a gift! It's an outrage! This life is not yours to give. You will never be welcomed here again."

Lydia heard Amie shriek, just one word. "Nooooo!" And then that, too, was swallowed by the sounds of the fairy revel.

"What about me?" Lydia asked as she and her mysterious companion landed on lush, soft, emerald green grass. "Can I go home?"

The fairy—they were too beautiful to be anything but a fairy—smiled, not answering, and led her deeper into the dance.

About

Kate Tomich

Kate Tomich is a writer and English teacher originally from the Chicago suburbs. She lives outside Beaverton, Oregon with her partner, two indoor cats, and numerous stray cats she feeds in her backyard. She spends her spare time art journaling, crafting, and dressing up in Renaissance clothes with her friends.

What inspired you to submit to "*Discover Beaverton*"?

A friend who is a guest editor for the publication mentioned the "Discover Beaverton" issue to our writing group, and I had an immediate idea pop into my head, so I ran with it. I'm a writer who dabbles in art, but for this issue I stuck with writing.

Was this your first time being published?

Yes.

What do you love about the piece you submitted?

I love that I finally had a chance to write about a location I pass by all the time and always think "there's a story down that pathway, I just know it!" I am excited that I finally got to put that little alleyway and those beautiful old buildings into a story. Readers who might not be too familiar with Beaverton should know that there are all sorts of wonderful old buildings and green spaces all around; it's not just the modern suburb it can look like from the freeway.

What's your favorite thing about Beaverton and/or Oregon?

My favorite thing about Oregon is the wild variety of places it holds. Oregon is full of amazing things that you could so easily miss if you're not here for a while. We have the world's smallest park, one of the largest urban forests in the world, and a landscape that goes from ocean to rivers to mountains to desert in a small enough space that you could visit them all on the same day.

What are you hoping readers take away from this issue?

There are odd and amazing places and spaces everywhere in Oregon, and Beaverton and the Portland Metro area are full of them, too. We have the world's smallest park and a Stonehenge replica not far outside Portland, one of the largest urban forests in the country, mountains, rivers, and the ocean close enough to see on the same day. And food...so many types of cuisine found in restaurants and food carts everywhere you turn. I hope readers will get a glimpse of the amazing mix of cultivated and wild blending into each other all through this place.

What does being a part of this project mean to you?

I love this project because it lets people see the close-up parts of a place, the things that someone there on the ground would see, not the long view you see on a map or a video or even in a travel article. This is a great chance to get to know a place from the inside.

WHAT COMMON THEMES HAVE YOU NOTICED? CHOOSE A POEM (OR STORY) FROM PAGES 12–54 & CONTINUE WRITING IT.

'23

High Tea Under the Dirigible Take 2

(Clockwork Rose Tea Emporium)

Marie Queen

What's your favorite thing about Beaverton and/or Oregon?

Clockwork Rose, Jan's Bookstore, Bubble n Tea, Patricia Reser Center for the Arts, the Round, Ava's Roasteria, the farmer's market, the city library, THPRD's nature parks...there are too many lovely places here to choose just one favorite spot! I think my favorite part about Beaverton is that you can visit so many fun and hip spots (all of the above, Shake Shack, Salt & Straw, etc.) and not even have to venture into Portland to get there. Yes, Beaverton is suburbia land but with a unique, charming, and diverse feel.

On a side note, my sporty tween daughter would tell you that being home to the Nike World Headquarters is the only thing that really counts, and I would say that the fact that they chose Beaverton means something!

What are you hoping readers take away from this issue?

I hope the readers/viewers will get a glimpse and appreciation of the enchantment of our small city.

What does being a part of this project mean to you?

I feel honored to be part of this project. This is my first time being published, and I am thrilled. I am proud of my Beaverton/Oregon roots and so happy to share my love for this city with others through my art.

ABOUT
DISCOVER BEAVERTON

With support from the **City of Beaverton Arts Program**, *Lucky Jefferson*'s *Discover Beaverton* is the first (to come) of future community-based anthologies that utilize ekphrastic-style story-telling to capture the brilliance of our everyday communities.

In this publication, you'll be delighted by poetry, fiction, creative nonfiction, and art that celebrate the uniqueness of Beaverton, Oregon!

Included writers and artists pay homage to Beaverton and invite those near and far to spark new connections to Beaverton.

Scan the code below to begin a new adventure:

DISCOVER BEAVERTON

a community anthology of poems, stories, and more by Lucky Jefferson

WRITE DOWN ONE THING YOU LEARNED ABOUT BEAVERTON THAT YOU DIDN'T KNOW BEFORE. USE THIS TO BEGIN A NEW POEM (OR STORY).

SUBMIT TO LUCKY JEFFERSON

***Lucky Jefferson*'s mission is simple: we publish social change.**

And our vision is to see books reimagined to center the modern reader.

Founded in 2018, *Lucky Jefferson* is an award-winning nonprofit, literary journal, and publisher that reimagines books by creating interactive and collaborative community experiences that center the writer and artist and cultivate inclusion and representation in contemporary literature.

Lucky Jefferson is proud to feature poets and writers who have never been published, marginalized perspectives, and those who sought to pursue writing later in life.

Learn more + consider submitting at: **luckyjefferson.com**

FOLLOW US

@LUCKY_JEFFERSON

@_LUCKYJEFFERSON

@LUCKYJEFFERSONLIT

STRIKE A POSE

TAKE A SELFIE
WITH YOUR COPY OF
DISCOVER BEAVERTON
AND TAG US!

HASHTAGSSSS

USE #DISCOVERBEAVERTON
OR #LJSQUAD TO
FOLLOW THE CONVO